P9-DMA-496

DORLING KINDERSLEY CLASSICS

GULLIVER'S TRAVELS

Dorling DK Kindersley

ADAPTED FOR YOUNG READERS

Produced by Leapfrog Press Ltd

Project Editor Slaney Begley
Art Editor Penny Lamprell
Picture Research Liz Moore

For Dorling Kindersley
Senior Editor Alastair Dougall
Managing Art Editor Jacquie Gulliver
Production Chris Avgherinos
DTP Designer Sue Wright

Published in the United States by Dorling Kindersley Publishing, Inc.
95 Madison Avenue, New York, New York 10016

First American Edition, 2000
2 468109 7531

Library of Congress Cataloging-in-Publication Data

Dunbar, James.
   Gulliver's travels / by Jonathan Swift ; adapted by James Dunbar.—1st American ed.
      p.cm. – (Dorling Kindersley classics)
   Summary: The voyages of an eighteenth-century Englishman carry him to such strange places as Lilliput,
where people are six inches tall, and Brobdingnag, a land peopled by giants. Illustrated notes throughout the
text explain the historical background of the story.
   ISBN 0-7894-5307-X
   [1. Voyages and travels—Fiction. 2. Fantasy.] I. Swift, Jonathan, 1667-1745. Gulliver's travels. II. Title. III.
Series.

PZ7.D8943 Gu 2000
[Fic]—dc21

99-043288

Color reproduction by Dot Gradations Limited
Printed by Graphicom in Italy

See our complete catalog at
www.dk.com

DORLING KINDERSLEY CLASSICS

GULLIVER'S TRAVELS

JONATHAN SWIFT

Adapted by
JAMES DUNBAR

Illustrated by
MARTIN HARGREAVES

A Dorling Kindersley Book

LONDON, NEW YORK, SYDNEY, DELHI, PARIS,
MUNICH and JOHANNESBURG

Contents

Lilliput

Brobdingnag

Laputa

*Land of the
Houyhnhnms*

INTRODUCTION

Although people of all ages have enjoyed reading *Gulliver's Travels* since it appeared in 1726, it was not written as a children's book. Instead, it was intended to make fun of many of the political, scientific, and educational events that took place during Jonathan Swift's lifetime. Readers in the 18th century would have been able to recognize many of the characters in the book, some of whom were only thinly disguised. Indeed, when it was first published it caused a scandal because it criticized the court and parliament. Today, however, we need information on the events taking place nearly 300 years ago to help explain what Swift was saying.

But *Gulliver's Travels* is not just a satire; it is also the gripping story of a fantastic voyage. As explorers pushed back the frontiers of the known world, tales of new countries peopled by strange and wonderful beings filtered back to Britain and the rest of Europe. Some of the stories were fact, and others, such as Daniel Defoe's *Robinson Crusoe*, were fiction. To try to make his story more believable, Lemuel Gulliver fills it with precise dates and exact measurements in the hope that he can fool the reader.

In many ways, Gulliver is a weak character whom few people like. He boasts a lot about how clever he is, yet he is always getting into trouble. When he finds his perfect community he is unable to stay there – and so he returns home, possibly crazy and hating everybody, including his family and friends.

Richard Harris as Lemuel Gulliver in the 1976 movie version.

In 1699 I accepted an appointment on the Antelope...bound for the South Sea.

bone saw

knife

Surgeon's tools

Surgery in the 17th century was a gruesome business. There were no anesthetics or antiseptics, so procedures were limited to simple, quick, or desperate operations, such as amputations. Sometimes, patients were given alcohol to drink before being held down and operated upon.

Chapter one

A VOYAGE TO LILLIPUT

MY FATHER HAD A SMALL ESTATE in Nottinghamshire; and I, Lemuel Gulliver, was the third of his five sons. I was sent to Cambridge University when I was fourteen and, after completing my studies there, I was apprenticed for four years to Mr. James Bates, a London surgeon. I had always longed to see the world, so during this time I also learned navigation. I then studied medicine in Leyden in Holland, knowing that this, too, would be useful on the voyages I felt destined to make.

My first appointment was as ship's surgeon on the *Swallow*. However, after three and a half years of voyaging, I resolved to settle in London. With the help of my good master Mr. Bates, I took up practice as a doctor; and, being advised to alter my status, I married Mary Burton, the second daughter of a hosier, who came with a dowry of four hundred pounds.

When Bates died, my practice began to fail, as my conscience would not let me adopt the medical malpractices of so many of my colleagues. After consulting my wife Mary, I again went to sea. I worked on various ships as a surgeon, voyaging to the East and

West Indies. During this time I read widely and observed the manners and customs of many peoples. Being blessed with an excellent memory, I also learned their languages.

In 1699, I accepted an appointment on the *Antelope*, and on May 4th we set sail from Bristol, bound for the South Sea. Our voyage proved prosperous until we were driven by a violent storm to the northwest of Van Diemen's Land. On November 5th our ship was dashed onto a rock and immediately split. Six of the crew, including myself, escaped in a longboat, but a huge wave soon swamped us. I never saw my companions again, and I believe they and all the rest of the crew must have perished.

I was swept by the wind and tide until my strength had gone. At last, just when I thought I could swim no more, I found I could touch the bottom with my feet. I walked for almost a mile before I reached the shore, and then continued inland for another half a mile in the hope of finding houses or inhabitants. It was evening, the storm had abated, and I was utterly exhausted. I lay down and slept more soundly than I had ever done before.

The East Indies
Swift uses actual places to make his story more realistic. Gulliver was heading for southeast Asia when he was shipwrecked off the northern coast of Australia.

English merchant ship
Ships such as the Antelope were called East Indiamen. They were used by the East India Company to import exotic cargo – including tea and coffee, silk and spices – to Europe.

Six of the crew, including myself, escaped in a longboat, but a huge wave soon swamped us.

When I awoke I tried to rise but could not move. I was firmly fastened to the ground – even my hair had been tied down. I was lying on my back and, as I could only look upward, the rising sun hurt my eyes. Suddenly I felt something alive on my left leg. It moved gradually up my body until it reached my chin.

It was a human, not six inches tall, armed with a bow and arrow.

By now I could feel at least forty such creatures on me. I roared so loudly that some fell off. I wrenched out the pegs that held my left arm; but the instant I tried to grab some of the little creatures I felt a shower of arrows, like needles, stick in my left hand.

I could hear crowds gathering. After a while some threads were cut, allowing me to turn my head to the right. Facing me, on a wooden stage, stood a man with two attendants, and a page boy no taller than my middle finger. This dignitary delivered a long speech of which I understood not a word. I replied humbly by gesturing with my free hand; and then I put my finger to my mouth, to show I was hungry.

The Hurgo (the title of a great lord, I learned later) understood my request. Ladders were lent against me and over a hundred people carried baskets of food to my mouth. I was fed joints of meat no larger than a lark's wing, and loaves of bread, which I ate three at a time. I then drank two barrels of wine, each holding barely half a pint.

Robinson Crusoe
Following the success of Daniel Defoe's Robinson Crusoe, *which was published in 1719–20, stories of being castaway in unknown lands became very popular.*

Immigration regulations
The Lilliputians represent the English. When they find Gulliver on the beach, they treat this large "illegal alien" with typical suspicion.

Later I was told that the wine had been mixed with a sleeping potion, and that was why I fell asleep. While I slept, nine hundred of their strongest men lifted me with pulleys, then lowered and tied me onto a specially made carriage. It took fifteen hundred horses, each about four and a half inches high, to transport me to their capital, about half a mile away.

About four hours after we set off, I was awakened by an officer in the guards, who stuck his half-pike up my left nostril, which tickled like a straw.

We traveled for the rest of the day, and, after stopping overnight, we arrived at the capital around noon the following day.

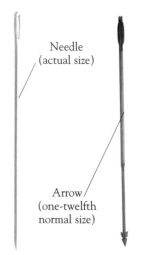

Needle
(actual size)

Arrow
(one-twelfth
normal size)

Scaled-down world
The Lilliputians' tiny bows fire needle-sized arrows. In general, people, animals, and objects in Lilliput are one-twelfth their normal size.

It was a human, not six inches tall, armed with a bow and arrow.

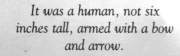

George I
The Emperor is probably based on King George I, who ruled England while Swift was writing. He was unpopular partly because he didn't speak good English (he was German). But Swift pokes fun at royal pride and tyranny in general in the character of the Emperor.

Just outside the city my carriage stopped at a disused temple. I was chained to its great door by my left leg so that I could do little more than stand, or creep inside what was now my lodgings.

The Emperor, his court, and over one hundred thousand inhabitants came to view me, and tens of thousands climbed ladders and clambered about me. The crowd gasped as I rose and looked around. Their countryside seemed like a garden, with fields no larger than flower beds, and woods where the tallest trees were only seven feet high. To my left was their city, which looked like the scenery in a theater.

From a safe distance the Emperor surveyed me with great admiration. I then lay down so that I could see them all more closely. The courtiers and ladies were magnificently clad, and the Emperor wore a gold helmet adorned with jewels and a plume.

His Majesty spoke to me, and I replied, but neither of us could understand a word.

When the court retired, I was left with a strong guard to protect me. While I sat by my house a few in the crowd had the impudence to fire arrows at me. As a punishment, the captain of the guard delivered the six ringleaders to me. I put five into my coat pocket, and I then threatened

I was chained to the disused temple by my left leg.

*His Majesty spoke to me, and I
replied, but neither of us could
understand a word.*

to eat alive the sixth. The poor man squealed terribly until I set him gently down, and away he ran. This I did with each prisoner in turn, and the crowd seemed relieved at my clemency.

My presence prompted much debate; there were fears of me breaking loose, or of my vast appetite causing a famine. Sometimes they decided to starve me, or shoot me in the face and hands with poisoned arrows. But this seemed no solution since it was felt that the stench of such a large carcass might cause a plague.

In the middle of these consultations, several army officers went to the council chamber to give an account of my merciful treatment of the prisoners. So his Majesty decreed that I should have food and drink. Six hundred servants were employed to wait on me, and scholars were appointed to teach me their language. His Majesty frequently honored me with visits. On each occasion I asked for my liberty, but was told to be patient.

The laws of Lilliput, for so the country I found myself in was named, required that I should be searched. The Emperor knew this could only be done with my consent, but he now had such confidence in me that he entrusted two officers into my care. I picked them up, firstly placing them in my coat pockets and then assisting them into others. They wrote an inventory of everything they found. At a later date I managed to translate this, word for word. They called me Quinbus Flestrin, or "Man Mountain."

In the right coat pocket of the great Man Mountain was a large piece of coarse cloth; large enough to be a carpet for your Majesty's state room.

In the left coat pocket we saw a huge silver chest. We desired it should be opened, and one of us stepping into it, found himself in a sort of dust which set us both a sneezing.

In the right waistcoat pocket was a folded bundle of white thin substance tied with cable, and marked with blacked figures; each figure half as large as the palm of our hands.

In the left waistcoat pocket was a sort of engine, from the back of which extended twenty long poles.

I picked them up, firstly placing them in my coat pockets and then assisting them into others.

In each of the large pockets of his breeches was a hollow pillar of iron, about the length of a man, fastened to a strong piece of timber.

In a smaller pocket were two black pillars. Within each of these was a prodigious steel plate.

There was a pocket we could not enter. It contained a wonderful globe from which hung a great silver chain. This engine made an incessant noise. He said he seldom did anything without consulting it, and it pointed out the time for every action of his life. So we assume it must be the god he worships.

Around the waist of Quinbus Flestrin hung a sword, the length of five men.

(signed)

Clefven Frelock

Marsi Frelock

Clefven Frelock,

Marsi Frelock.

When this inventory was read to the Emperor, he ordered my sword and pocket pistols to be taken away by carriage. Everything else I was allowed to keep. I had one private pocket which I did not reveal, as it only housed my spectacles, a spy-glass, and a few things that would be of no consequence to the Emperor.

Gulliver's Possessions
Our hero has so many things in his pockets it is a wonder he didn't sink like a stone during the shipwreck!
Gulliver's possessions are typical of an 18th-century traveler. One of the items that causes the Lilliputians most surprise is his snuff box. Taking snuff had been fashionable in Europe since the 1670s and boxes often had elaborate designs. Another is Gulliver's pocket watch – clearly the Lilliputians are not very mechanically minded.

Iron-framed spectacles, c.1750

Double-barreled pocket pistol, c.1780

Spy-glass, c.1750

Pocket watch, c.1720

Sir Robert Walpole
Flimnap, the Emperor's nimble Treasurer, is thought to be a caricature of the politician Sir Robert Walpole (1676–1745). Walpole was a master player of political power games, and held office for a record 21 years.

garter

Order of the Garter
In this passage, Swift satirizes the British honors system. He describes the Order of the Garter– whose members wore a star, a garter below the left knee, and a blue ribbon – as well as lesser orders.

Sedan chair
Aristocrats would often travel short distances within cities in a sedan chair. These enclosed seats for one passenger were carried on poles by two bearers. They were a common sight in the 17th and 18th centuries.

I hoped that soon I might be granted my liberty. My good behavior was well received by the Emperor; and through my gentleness everyone became less fearful of me. I would sometimes lie down and let five or six of the people dance on my hand, or their children play hide and seek in my hair.

One day the Emperor invited me to watch the Rope Dance. This ceremony is performed on a slender thread about two feet long and twelve inches above the ground. Anyone seeking high office at court has to display their agility on this rope. The successful candidate is the one who jumps the highest without falling off. I saw two or three break a limb, and records show that accidents are often fatal. Sometimes chief ministers have to perform on the rope to reassure the Emperor that they are still capable of holding office. Flimnap, the Treasurer, can still cut a caper at least one inch higher than anyone else; and I have even seen him do somersaults.

Anyone seeking high office at Court has to display their agility on this rope.

There is also a diversion known as Leaping and Creeping, by which the Emperor grants royal favors. His Majesty holds out a stick while candidates, one by one, either jump over it, or crawl forward and backward under it; depending on whether the stick is raised or lowered. Whoever survives the longest is honored with a blue silk belt; the second a red and the third a green. I noticed that most great persons at Court display one of these colors.

One day I constructed a square of poles about two feet high, by driving tree trunks firmly into the ground. I then fastened my handkerchief to these poles until it was as tight as a drum. With his Majesty's approval, I placed some of his best horsemen on this plain. From here they paraded before the Emperor and performed a mock battle. He was so delighted that he ordered the entertainment to be repeated several days later, and even persuaded the Empress herself to let me hold her in her close chair within two yards of the stage.

While entertaining the Court I was interrupted with a message that a large black object, oddly shaped and rising in the middle to the height of a man, had been found lying on the shore. When it was brought to me, dragged over the ground by five horses, I realized that they had found my hat.

Tricorn hat
During Swift's lifetime, all gentlemen would have worn wigs and would not have considered going out without a hat. Tricorns were cocked hats that had the brim turned up on three sides.

With his Majesty's approval, I placed some of his best horsemen on this plain.

Two days after the return of my hat, the Emperor planned an unusual diversion for his army. He asked me to stand like a colossus, with my legs astride, while his troops marched under me. Three thousand foot soldiers at twenty-four abreast, and one thousand cavalry at sixteen, marched beneath me with drums beating and colors flying.

In time his Majesty, in full council, agreed to grant me my freedom. Only one minister voted against: Skyresh Bolgolam, the Galbet or Admiral, who without any provocation chose to be my enemy.

I willingly agreed to my Articles of Freedom and took the oath according to their laws. I had to hold my right foot in my left hand, while placing the middle finger of my right hand on the crown of my head, and my thumb on the tip of my right ear. In this manner I swore to the following conditions:

1. *The Man Mountain shall not leave Lilliput without permission.*
2. *He shall not enter our capital without permission; the inhabitants shall have two hours warning to keep indoors.*
3. *He shall confine his walks to the highways, and not walk or lie down in a meadow or field.*
4. *He shall take the utmost care not to trample upon any of our loving subjects, nor pick up any subject without their consent.*
5. *He shall assist with urgent dispatches, by carrying the messenger and his horse.*
6. *He shall be our ally against our enemies in the Island of Blefuscu.*
7. *He shall, at times, assist our men in their work by lifting great stones.*
8. *He shall make an accurate survey of our island's coastline.*
9. *Lastly, on his agreeing to these conditions, he shall be given a daily allowance of food sufficient for the support of 1,728 of our subjects.*

It may interest the reader to know how my daily allowance had been calculated. His Majesty's mathematicians measured my height with a quadrant, and found it exceeded theirs in proportion of twelve to one. So they concluded that, as our bodies were similar, mine must contain at least 1,728 of theirs.

Colossus of Rhodes
This bronze statue of the sun god Helios or Apollo was one of the Seven Wonders of the Ancient World. It was probably over 100 feet (30 meters) high, and may have been built bestriding the harbor so that ships could pass beneath its legs. Today, "colossus" is used to describe something that is large.

Three thousand foot soldiers at twenty-four abreast, and one thousand cavalry at sixteen, marched beneath me with drums beating and colors flying.

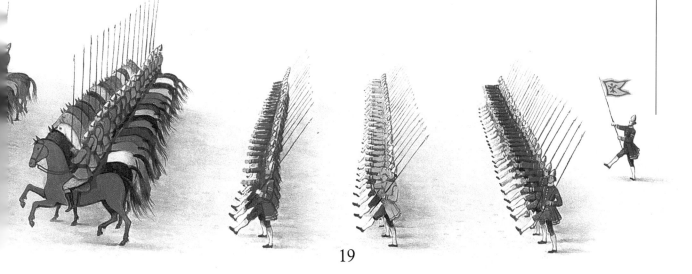

Whigs and Tories
The Whigs (low heels) and the Tories (high heels) were the two main political parties in Britain from the late 17th to the 19th century. The Whigs were in power when Gulliver's Travels was written.

Religious differences
Swift mocked Catholics (Big-Endians) and Protestants (Little-Endians) for warring over religious differences.

Now that I was free, his Majesty allowed me to visit Mildendo, the capital of Lilliput. I stepped over the great Western Gate and walked down the main street, while crowds looked on from upper windows. Everyone had been ordered to stay indoors, but I was still mindful of treading on stragglers.

His Majesty was eager for me see the magnificence of his palace, in the center of Mildendo. With great dexterity I reached the royal apartments and lay down. Through the open windows of the splendid royal rooms I saw the Empress, and the young Princes. Her Majesty smiled graciously and even gave me her hand to kiss. I shall say no more of the palace, as I shall give a full description in my greater work on Lilliput, soon to be published.

About a fortnight later, the Principal Secretary, Reldresal, was sent by the Emperor to tell me about two great evils that threatened Lilliput.

"For seventy moons," Reldresal began, "we have had two opposing parties in Lilliput: the Tramecksans and Slamecksans, who distinguish themselves by wearing either high or low heels on their shoes. There are more Tramecksans, as high heels are the tradition. Although there are fewer of us, the Slamecksans hold the power, as this Emperor favors low heels. The feelings between our two parties are so bad that we do not even talk to each other. What makes matters worse is that the heir to the throne now wears one heel higher than the other, showing a possible leaning toward the Tramecksans.

"In the midst of this civil unrest," Reldresal continued, "we are now threatened with invasion by the Island of Blefuscu. This bloody and costly conflict started thirty-six moons ago. The son of a previous Emperor cut his finger while breaking his boiled egg at the big end. His father decreed that all eggs must, in future, be broken at the smaller end. This law has been so resented that it has caused six rebellions, with eleven thousand Big-Endians preferring to die rather than break their eggs at the smaller end. Blefuscu has always encouraged these Big-Endians and grants them sanctuary. I tell you all this because his Majesty has great confidence in your courage and loyalty to Lilliput."

I told Reldresal to assure the Emperor that I would defend him and his people against all invaders.

With great dexterity
I reached the royal
apartments and
lay down.

French navy

The Island of Blefuscu is a portrait of France, and the hostilities between Lilliput (Britain) and Blefuscu mimic the War of the Spanish Succession (1702–13). Since sea battles were often decided by freak weather conditions, sailors were extremely superstitious. Tales such as this one, of a giant emerging from the depths and capturing the fleet, were commonplace.

I drew fifty of the enemy's largest men-of-war after me with great ease.

The islands of Lilliput and Blefuscu are separated by a channel eight hundred yards wide and, at its deepest, seventy glumgluffs (about six feet). I told his Majesty of my plan for seizing the Blefuscudian invasion fleet. From some iron bars, the size of knitting needles, I made fifty hooks. I tied each hook to a length of cable, no thicker than thread. I then went to the coast and, taking off my outer garments, I waded into the sea. Within half an hour I arrived at the enemy's ships. My sudden appearance so frightened the sailors that they jumped overboard.

I fastened a hook to each warship and tied the ends of cable into one knot. All the while the enemy fired thousands of arrows into my hands and face. I then cut the ships from their anchors and, taking the knot in my hand, began to pull. I drew fifty of the enemy's largest men-of-war after me with great ease. When out of danger I stopped to pick out the arrows. Then I waded back to Lilliput with my cargo and was welcomed with great ceremony. His Majesty immediately

Louis XIV
*France became the most
formidable kingdom in
Europe under Louis XIV
(1638–1715), who was
known as the Sun King. As
France began to extend her
borders, countries such as
Britain felt threatened and
declared war.*

created me a Nardac,
the highest of their honors.

The Emperor wanted to take this opportunity to
conquer Blefuscu and destroy all the Big-Endian exiles.
I refused to take part in reducing these free people into
slavery, and later expressed an intention to visit them.
The Emperor never forgave me for the compassion I showed
toward the Blefuscudians.

One night I was woken by cries of "*Burglum!*" ("Fire!") and
hurried to the palace. Her Majesty's apartments were on fire
and would have been destroyed if I had not, that evening,
been drinking a delicious wine called *glimigrim*. I now felt
the need to discharge myself of it, and directed myself so
accurately onto the flames that the fire was extinguished. Yet,
to my dismay, this won me no favors with the Emperor, while
the Empress, in her disgust, refused to return to her rooms,
and vowed revenge for the insult she felt I had done her.

*I directed myself so
accurately onto the
flames that the fire
was extinguished.*

My position with the Emperor declined still further when
he heard my stay had cost his treasury over a million and a
half *sprugs* (their highest gold coin). Flimnap, the Lord High
Treasurer, always spoke ill of me, perhaps because he was
only a Clumglum, a title inferior to a Nardac.

SUMATRA

Blefuscu

Lilliput

Mildendo

ALL ABOUT LILLIPUT

Lilliput is an island to the southwest of Sumatra and the Sunda Straits and northwest of Cape Van Dieman. Blefuscu is an island to the northeast of Lilliput. The two islands are separated by a channel that is 800 yards (730 meters) wide and 6 feet (1.8 meters or 70 glumguffs) at the deepest point. The capital city of Lilliput is Mildendo, while the capital of Blefuscu is also called Blefuscu. Both Lilliput and Blefuscu are ruled by Emperors, who have the power to appoint their governments.

Mildendo – capital of Lilliput

Mildendo is about ½ mile (800 meters) from the coast. It is surrounded by walls 2½ feet (75 cm) high and 11 in (28 cm) thick. The wall is interrupted by a stout tower every 10 feet (3 meters). Gulliver entered the city by stepping over the Western Gate. The city is an exact square, each side being 500 feet (150 meters) long. Two main streets divide the city into four square sections, and each section is subdivided by alleyways. In 1699, Mildendo had a population of about 500,000.

Western Gate

Emperor's palace

two- and three- story houses

tower

Southern Gate

Emperor

The Lilliputian's emperor is taller than any of his subjects, and is described by Gulliver as having strong, masculine features, an olive complexion, and a well-proportioned body. In the story he is 28¾ and had ruled for 7 years.

Legal System

The Lilliputian legal system is based on the theory that the better you behave, the more you are rewarded. To symbolize this, the statue of Justice has a sheathed sword in her left hand, indicating no punishment; in her right hand she holds a bag of coins, symbolizing reward for obedience. Any Lilliputian who can show that he or she has obeyed the laws for 73 moons is granted privileges paid for by the State, and also receives the non-hereditary title of Snilpall.

Education

Lilliputians take the view that a child has no reason to be grateful to his or her parents for being born – birth is nature's way of continuing the species. Lilliputians also think that parents are the last people to be entrusted with the development of their children, so there are public nurseries in every area.

A Lilliputian family

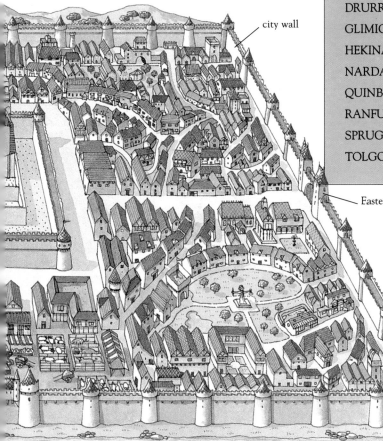

city wall

Eastern Gate

THE LILLIPUTIAN LANGUAGE

Despite speaking several languages fluently, Gulliver found the Lilliputian language quite unlike any other he had come across. It was even more difficult to understand when written down. Although Gulliver was given tuition and was able to translate Lilliputian, only a few words were recorded by him.

A page of Lilliputian writing (actual size)

BORACH MIVOLAH!	*"LOOK OUT!"*
CLUMGLUM	*one rank below Nardac*
DRURR	*measure of length*
GLIMIGRIM	*delicious sort of wine*
HEKINAH DEGUL!	*"Wow" or "that's amazing"*
NARDAC	*highest rank in Lilliput*
QUINBUS FLESTRIN	*Man-Mountain (name given to Gulliver)*
RANFU-LO	*pants, trousers, breeches*
SPRUG	*currency used in Blefuscu*
TOLGO PHONAC	*order given before firing arrows*

RELATIVE SIZES IN LILLIPUT

The inhabitants of Lilliput are perfectly formed humans, but only 6 inches (15 cm or 84 drurrs in Lilliputian measure) tall when fully grown. Everything is about one-twelfth the size it would be in our world, so it is on a scale of approximately 1 inch to 1 foot. Their tallest trees are 7 feet (2 meters) high and can be found in the great royal park outside Mildendo. The biggest horses and cows are 4–5 inches (10–13 cm) high, and sheep are about 1½ inches (4 cm) tall. Their geese are the size of our sparrows, while their smallest birds are almost too small for Gulliver to see.

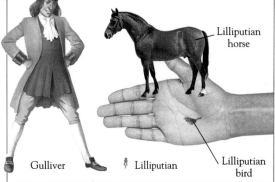

Lilliputian horse

Gulliver

Lilliputian

Lilliputian bird

Funeral rites

The Lilliputians bury their dead vertically and upside down, so that the corpse's feet are the nearest part of the body to the surface. They believe that the earth is flat, and that in 11,000 moons' time it will turn upside down. When this happens, the dead will be the right way up for resurrection; indeed they should be standing on their own two feet. The more educated Lilliputians think this idea is absurd, but they still do it.

A Lilliputian funeral

High treason
Convicted criminals were sometimes put to death in horrible ways. High treason, which meant plotting against the state (including the king or queen), was the gravest of all crimes. Until 1814 those found guilty of high treason were hanged, cut down when they were still alive, and disembowelled. Their bodies were then cut into quarters, beheaded, and burned.

Out of gratitude for favors I had done for him, he had come to warn me.

Late one night a high official came to my house secretly, in a closed chair and without announcing his name. Out of gratitude for favors I had done for him, he had come to warn me.

"His Majesty, within the past two days, has agreed a resolution accusing you of high treason. As you must know, you have some influential enemies at court. Skyresh Bolgolam and Flimnap, for their own personal motives, have drafted an indictment against you, and I have managed to procure a copy.

"I will read you the more serious of their charges:

"*Articles of Impeachment against* Quinbus Flestrin (*the Man-Mountain*). *Firstly, in contravention of an ancient statute, he did maliciously, and devilishly, discharge his urine within the palace precincts. Secondly, he traitorously refused to assist his Majesty to become Emperor of Blefuscu and put to death all Big-Endian exiles.* There are further charges of showing compassion for enemy subjects and traitorously intending to visit Blefuscu.

"There has been much discussion about your punishment. Your enemies suggest a most painful and ignominious death; by setting fire to your house at night, then shooting you with poisoned arrows; or by rubbing your clothes with poison that would make you tear your flesh and die in utmost torture. However, his Majesty wishes to appear lenient to the world. So your official punishment is to have both your eyes put out, but, in truth, they afterward intend to slowly starve you to death. I leave it to you what action you take. I must now go, as secretly as I came."

After some thought, I wrote to Principal Secretary Reldresal. I said nothing of this warning, but innocently informed the court that I intended to visit Blefuscu.

I will not trouble the reader with a detailed account of my reception in Blefuscu. I told his Majesty that I was honoring my intention to visit his empire, and he welcomed me generously. Three days later, I noticed an upturned, full-sized boat about half a league out to sea. With the help of two thousand men I brought it near to shore, turned it over, and found it was little damaged.

Public hangings
Some 200 crimes in Britain were punishable by death at the time Swift was writing, although only about one in three sentences was actually carried out. Hangings and bloody beatings were often carried out in public, and were popular attractions.

*Three days later,
I noticed an upturned,
full-sized boat about half a
league out to sea.*

I told the Emperor of Blefuscu that it was good fortune that had brought me such a prodigious boat. Now I might have a chance of reaching my home country. He granted me help to make my vessel seaworthy, and gave me sufficient food for my voyage. I stored my boat with the carcasses of a hundred oxen and three hundred sheep, together with bread and drink. I took with me six live cows and two bulls, with as many ewes and rams, for breeding. His Majesty trusted me not to carry away any of his subjects, even if they wished to come with me.

On September 24th, 1701, I set sail; I had been here just ten months and nineteen days. On my third day at sea I was picked up by an English merchantman, returning from Japan. I put my cows and my sheep in my pockets, and my heart leapt as I went on board. The captain asked where I had been last, and I explained to him as briefly as I could. He thought I was raving until I took the cattle and sheep out of my pocket and some other rarities of those islands. He then, very clearly, believed me.

He thought I was raving until I took the cattle and sheep out of my pocket.

The rest of my livestock I set to graze on a bowling green at Greenwich.

We arrived in England on April 13th, 1702. On the journey I had the misfortune to have one of my sheep eaten by the ship's rats. The rest of my livestock I set to graze on a bowling green at Greenwich, and made some profit by showing them off.

I stayed about two months with my wife, my son Johnny, and daughter Betty. But my insatiable desire to travel to foreign countries forced me to return to sea. There were tears on both sides as I boarded the *Adventure*, a merchantman. On June 20th, 1702 I set sail for Surat. I shall give an account of this voyage in the second part of my travels.

There were tears on both sides as I boarded the Adventure.

Poor Jack

The popular ballad on this jug describes how difficult long sea voyages were on the families left behind. Wives had to run their households without a regular income, and children did not see their fathers for months and sometimes years at a time.

Chapter two

A VOYAGE TO BROBDINGNAG

O UR VOYAGE WAS FAIR until we reached the Straits of Madagascar. From here we were driven eastward by storms until even the oldest sailor on board could not tell in what part of the world we were. On June 16th, 1703 we sighted land, and the following day I went ashore in the longboat with a dozen men.

While the men searched for fresh water, I went off alone to spy out the land. Finding nothing of much interest – the landscape was barren and rocky – I soon decided to turn back. As I strolled along the beach toward the place where we had landed, I was astonished to see that the men had put to sea without me and were rowing for their lives. I was about to call after them when I saw a huge creature striding through the waves. They had half a league start and, as the sea was full of sharp rocks, the creature was forced to turn back. I ran from the shore and climbed a hill. From there I saw a countryside of fields, but what amazed me was the size of everything – the grass was twenty feet high.

The hedge around a cornfield was over one hundred and twenty feet high and the corn was at least forty feet tall. I walked an hour in this field, until I saw seven creatures cutting the corn with huge scythes coming toward me. Each was as tall as a church steeple and took ten yards at every stride. One of the reapers was so near I expected his next step would squash me.

I screamed as loud as fear would let me. The giant paused and looked around. At last he saw me lying terrified on the ground and picked me up between his thumb and forefinger. As I was at least sixty feet in the air I resolved not to struggle though he pinched my sides terribly. He ran immediately with me to his master, the farmer.

The farmer prodded me with a straw, then blew my hair aside to see my face. I took off my hat and gave him a bow, then fell on my knees and lifted my hands as if begging for mercy. He spoke in a deafening noise and I answered as loudly as I could.

Although we could not understand each other, he realized I must be a rational creature. He wrapped me up in his handkerchief and carried me home. When his wife saw me, she screamed as if she had seen a spider.

At last he saw me lying terrified on the ground and picked me up.

At about noon, the farmer, his wife, and three children sat down to eat. I was placed on the table but kept well away from the edge in case I fell the thirty feet to the floor. The wife crumbled me some bread and gave me a

The farmer's son, about ten years old, grabbed me by the legs and held me high in the air.

drink. When I shouted my thanks, as loud as I could, the company laughed so heartily I was almost deafened. The farmer's son, about ten years old, grabbed me by the legs and held me high in the air, but his father snatched me from him and gave him a blow on the left ear that would have felled a troop of horsemen. Worried that the boy might bear a grudge against me, and remembering how mischievous our children often are toward sparrows, rabbits, kittens, and puppy dogs, I fell on my knees and, pointing to the boy, made my master understand that I desired his son should be pardoned. I then kissed the boy's hand, which my master took, and made him stroke me gently with it.

During dinner my mistress's cat leapt into her lap. It was three times larger than an ox, and I stood at the far end of the table, about fifty feet away, fearing it might pounce. However, it showed no interest in me. I was less fearful of the dogs around the table, even though one was a mastiff equal in bulk to four elephants.

When dinner was almost done the nurse came in with a year-old child. As soon as the babe spied me it bellowed to have me as a toy. The mother out of pure indulgence placed me near the child, who immediately put my head in its mouth. I roared so loudly that it dropped me. Fortunately I fell into the mother's apron.

Being on the table I had a close view of these people. The sight of their complexions reminded me of a time in Lilliput when I was told that, close to, my face was a shocking sight with great holes in the skin and bristles stronger than a boar's. I should add that I am as good looking as most men from my country and my face has not been burned by the sun, despite my travels. So, in fairness to this race, I will merely say that they are comely and well proportioned, even though I found everything about them vast in size.

When dinner was over, my mistress put me on her bed and covered me with a handkerchief larger and coarser than a ship's mainsail. And there I slept.

Tom Thumb
In Brobdingnag, Gulliver must have felt like Tom Thumb, the well-known fairy-tale character. Swift would have been told stories about the tiny hero as a child, and would later have read of his exploits.

Dolls

Like today, many girls in the 18th century enjoyed playing with dolls – giving them characters and making them clothes and houses. Glumdalclitch must have been delighted when Gulliver came to live with her family, as to her he really was a "living doll."

Two rats crept up the curtains and onto the bed.

I dreamt I was at home with my wife and children. This made my sadness even greater when I awoke on a bed twenty yards wide, in a room two hundred feet high. Two rats crept up the curtains and onto the bed. They were the size of mastiffs but far more agile. I jumped up and drew my sword as they attacked me. I killed one, and wounded the other as it fled. Soon after, my mistress came into the room and was very relieved to find I was not hurt.

My mistress had a nine-year-old daughter and together they fitted up her doll's cradle as my bed. The girl was skillful at making me clothes, and she also taught me their language. She called me Grildrig, or "manikin"; I called her my Glumdalclitch, or "little nurse." She was very good-natured, and not above forty feet high, and it is to her that I owe my safety, as we never parted while I was in this country.

It was soon the talk of the neighborhood that my master had found a strange animal in the fields, a human being about the size of a *splacknuck* (one of the country's animals that was about six feet long). On the advice of a fellow farmer, my master decided to exhibit me. Glumdalclitch was heartbroken at such an indignity, and feared I might be mishandled or even killed.

Next market day I was taken to town in a box that had been given a door and air holes. My "little nurse" had lined it with a doll's quilt, but even so I was very shaken by the journey. My master hired a room at the inn and advertised me as a spectacle. I performed on a table while Glumdalclitch stayed near; I recited speeches, toasted the crowd, and flourished my sword as if I were fencing. After eight hours of this routine I was too tired to stand or talk.

Even when at home I had no rest. Each day, groups came to the house and paid to watch me. My master, realizing the profit he would make, decided to show me throughout the kingdom. So, within two months of my arrival, he set out for the city with Glumdalclitch; and me traveling in a box tied around her waist.

Freak shows
People who were unusually tall or small, or who had some other sort of disability, were often exhibited as freaks at country shows or outside pubs. This 16th-century girl, who was covered in hair, would have been treated as a great curiosity.

I recited speeches, toasted the crowd, and flourished my sword as if I were fencing.

On the 26th of October we arrived at the capital, Lorbrulgrud, or "Pride of the Universe." My master hired a room where I gave ten performances each day. The more popular I became, the more greedy the farmer grew, and I was forced to work even harder until I was little more than a skeleton. Within a few weeks my health began to suffer and my master, suspecting that I might soon die, made me work even harder.

The Queen had heard such good reports of my abilities, behavior, and wit that we were summoned to the royal palace. I fell on my knees and begged the honor of kissing her imperial foot. But the Gracious Empress asked my master whether he would sell me and, after I was set on a table, held out her little finger, which I embraced with both my arms and kissed. He, who thought I may not live the month, was eager to part with me for one thousand pieces of gold. Glumdalclitch, who was so caring and kind, stayed with me. In the presence of such a great and good Empress I found that my health and spirits soon revived.

Protective women
Gulliver owes his survival in Brobdingnag to two women – Glumdalclitch and the Queen. The men he meets either ignore him or try to exploit him.

The Gracious Empress held out her little finger, which I embraced with both my arms and kissed.

*After three weeks,
my home was built
and I moved in.*

Unlike the Queen, his Majesty had a more severe disposition. At first he suspected I was an ingenious piece of clockwork, and three of his Majesty's scholars were consulted about my origins. They agreed that I could not have evolved according to the normal laws of nature: I was too insignificant and not equipped for self-preservation, either in hunting or defense. I was not an embryo, as I had perfectly formed limbs and the stubble of a beard. Also, I was not a dwarf, as the Queen's favorite was the smallest ever known, and he was near thirty feet tall. They concluded that I was a *Relpum Scalcath* – one of nature's little jokes.

The Queen ordered her craftsman to make me a home. Glumdalclitch and myself designed a wooden chamber with windows, a door and two rooms. The ceiling lifted up so that furniture could be added. The inside was quilted to prevent injury while I was being carried by its handles, or taken by coach. After three weeks, my home was built and I moved in.

Gulliver's personality
Gulliver is a terrible snob who is hugely impressed by royalty, and loves the attention he receives from "the Gracious Empress." He also loves to be praised, and never fails to tell the reader how intelligent, witty, and well-mannered he is.

In all my time in Brobdingnag, nothing angered me more than the attitude of the Queen's dwarf. He took to swaggering and looking big whenever he saw me, and usually made some smart remark about my littleness. One day at dinner this malicious little creature was so nettled by something I had said that he dropped me into a bowl of cream. Glumdalclitch spooned me out uninjured, except for a spoilt suit. The dwarf was soundly whipped, and soon after left the court.

The dwarf had always shown me resentment. His usual trick had been to catch flies and then release them in my face. I found these odious insects particularly loathsome as, to me, they were the size of birds. A fly would land on my food and I could see it, all too visibly, leave its excrement or spawn behind. But there were also times when I provoked the dwarf's resentment. Once Glumdalclitch left me under a dwarf apple tree, and when the dwarf came near I made some silly comment about his name and that of the tree. He shook the tree so hard that apples, bigger than beer barrels, tumbled around me; and one knocked me flat.

The malicious little creature dropped me into a bowl of cream.

Famous royal dwarf
This portrait shows Queen Henrietta Maria, the wife of Charles I, with her court dwarf "Sir" Jeffrey Hudson (1619–82). Hudson was 3 feet 9 inches (114 cm) tall. The son of a butcher, he became Captain of the Horse.

Apples, bigger than beer barrels, tumbled around me.

My littleness often exposed me to troublesome or ridiculous accidents. One breakfast time, as I was eating some cake, twenty wasps invaded my house, humming louder than bagpipes. They were the size of partridges but I killed four with my sword before the rest flew off. I carefully removed their one-and-a-half-inch stings, and kept them as curios.

Twenty wasps invaded my house, humming louder than bagpipes.

The garden was a particularly vulnerable place for me. In a sudden shower I was severely bruised by hailstones the size of tennis balls. Another time the gardener's spaniel took me in his teeth. Fortunately he had been well taught and carried me, without the least hurt, straight to his master. I have also fallen through a mole hill up to my neck, and injured my ankle on a snail shell.

The Queen, who listened to me talk about my voyages, had a boat made for me. I would show off my water skills in a large trough, and sometimes I would put up the sail and the court ladies would create a breeze with their fans. On one occasion a frog jumped onto my boat, almost capsizing me. It would not leave until I had struck it many times with my oar. But my worst danger was yet to happen.

The Queen, who listened to me talk about my voyages, had a boat made for me.

One day, when Glumdalclitch had left me in her room, a pet monkey belonging to one of the Clerks of the Kitchen sprang in through the window. From my house I could see it leaping around the room. Then it noticed my box, which it seemed to view with great curiosity, peeping in through the door and every window. I tried to remain hidden, but, after some frisking and chattering, it saw me, put its paw into my house and dragged me out by my coat collar. At the sound of Glumdalclitch returning, my captor leapt through the window and scrambled onto the roof with its prize.

Many of the court gathered below; some were even amused by the monkey trying to feed me with chewed-up food from its mouth. When the monkey spied my rescuers on ladders, it ran off, abandoning me on the roof, three hundred yards above the ground. I sat there, too terrified to move, until a young footman climbed up, put me in his breeches pocket, and brought me down.

When later the King teased me about this incident, I tried to explain that, in my country, monkeys were not usually the size of elephants, but in the same proportion to me as this monkey was to him. The King merely laughed.

There was another time the court laughed at my expense. On a walk in the country, I attempted to jump over a cowpat, but landed in the middle, up to my knees in dung. I waded out with some difficulty and was wiped down by a footman.

On two occasions I tried to show my gratitude for their Majesties' favors and protection. One time, I was allowed some of her Majesty's hair from her comb. I wove the hair so as to form the seats and backs on two chair frames. When I presented the chairs to her Majesty as curios she asked me to sit on one. However I absolutely refused to place a dishonorable part of myself on those precious hairs that had once adorned her Majesty's head.

The King was very fond of music, and fortunately I had some skill on the spinet, which I had learned to play in my youth.

My captor scrambled onto the roof with its prize.

Lady and pet monkey
Exotic pets were popular during the 16th, 17th, and 18th centuries, and would have been seen at most European courts. This portrait shows the Infanta Isabella Clara Eugenia, the daughter of Philip II of Spain, with her pet monkey.

There was a spinet in Glumdalclitch's room, so I decided to entertain their Majesties with an English tune. This proved extremely difficult as the spinet was nearly sixty foot long and each of its keys a foot wide. I could barely reach five keys with my arms outstretched. The solution I came up with was to make two beaters and run up and down the keyboard as fast as I could, banging the proper notes. It was the most violent exercise I ever underwent.

Another time, I told his Majesty about a powder that exploded like thunder and could drive a metal ball with speed and great violence. I explained how the largest balls could destroy whole lines of men or sink ships, and that sometimes we compressed this powder into large hollow balls of iron and then discharged them into cities, destroying houses and injuring all who were near. I humbly offered my knowledge of this invention to his Majesty.

The King was struck with horror that so feeble and groveling an insect as I (his own words) should entertain such inhuman ideas. I was ordered never to mention that powder again.

Spinet
This keyboard instrument is one of the smallest members of the harpsichord family. The spinet would have been found in many homes prior to the 19th century, when the piano became more popular.

Canons
The king of Brobdingnag is astonished and shocked to discover that Gulliver's tiny countrymen are so warlike. He is also horrified to hear of a weapon – the cannon – that is capable of such mass destruction.

It was the most violent exercise I ever underwent.

ALL ABOUT BROBDINGNAG

Brobdingnag is a large peninsula on the coast of California, discovered in 1703 by Lemuel Gulliver. It is 6,000 miles (9,650 km) long and between 3,000 and 5,000 miles (4,800 and 8,000 km) wide. To the northeast it is cut off by a range of volcanic mountains, some of them 30 miles (48 km) high. No one knows what kind of people, if any, live on the other side of the mountains. The rest of the country is surrounded by the Pacific Ocean. There is no sea-fishing in Brobdingnag because the coastline is very rocky and the waters are extremely rough. However, there are plenty of large fish in the country's inland rivers. Brobdingnag is well inhabited: there are 51 cities, 100 walled towns, and a great number of villages.

Flanflasnic

Lorbrulgrud

Brobdingnag

NORTH AMERICA

RELATIVE SIZES IN BROBDINGNAG

The inhabitants of Brobdingnag are a race of giants as tall as church steeples. They cover 9 meters (10 yards) with one stride. All things in their country are in proportion – corn is 40 feet (12 meters) high, rats are the size of large dogs, and flies are the size of larks. The hailstones are 18 times larger than any other known hailstones. Huge bones dug up in various parts of the country suggest that the ancestors of the Brobdingnags were even larger.

fly

Brobdingnagian   Gulliver   rat   corn

Lorbrulgrud – capital of Brobdingnag

Lorbrulgrud (meaning "Pride of the Universe") stands in the center of the country. It is divided into two parts, separated by a river. The most important monument is the temple tower, 3,000 feet (900 meters) high, with walls 100 feet (30 meters) thick.

The royal palace

The King and Queen's primary residence in Lorbrulgrud is about 7 miles (11 km) round. The state rooms are generally 240 feet (73 meters) high. At the time, European palaces such as Versailles were being built on a grand scale.

The Palace of Versailles

temple tower

Political history

In the recent past there has been a struggle for power between the King, the Nobility, and his people. This has led to several civil wars, the last ending in the signing of a general treaty. The monarchy is founded on common sense, reason, justice, and leniency.

Gulliver before the King and Queen of Brobdingnag

Laws

Brobdingnag's laws are simple and clear. None of them may exceed in words the number of letters in the alphabet, and they must be expressed in clear, simple language. Murder is a capital offense and murderers are beheaded.

Glumdalclitch Graltrud slpacknuk relplum scalcath
Glumdalclitch Graltrud slpacknuk relplum scalcath
Glumdalclitch Graltrud slpacknuk relplum scalcath

CULTURE IN BROBDINGNAG

Brobdingnagians study morality, history, mathematics, and poetry. They have been able to print books since early times, but their libraries are not comprehensive. The King has the largest library of 1,000 volumes in a gallery 1,200 feet (365 meters) long. Some books are 20 feet (6 meters) long.

Gulliver took 8–10 paces per line when reading a book in Brobdingnag.

royal palace

Army

There are 32,000 cavalry and 176,000 infantrymen in the Brobdingnagian army. Soldiers are drawn from city traders and country farmers. The commanders are all members of the aristocracy and are unpaid. Gunpowder is unknown and so there are no guns or cannons in warfare.

Swords were the main weapons in Brobdingnag

river

Sinbad the Sailor
This section of Gulliver's Travels *is similar to one of Sinbad's seven adventures in* The Arabian Nights. *In it, the hero is carried away by a fabulous white bird of great size and strength, known as the Roc.*

I had now been two years in this country and always had the belief that I would find my freedom. I was missing my own people; and the King was also on the lookout for creatures like myself. However, I suspected that his intention was to propagate our species to sell as curios, like caged canaries.

The King and Queen made a visit to their palace near the city of Flanflasnic, on the southern coast. On arrival I was impatient to see the ocean and, as Glumdalclitch was ill, she entrusted me to a page. The lad carried me to the shore and placed my box so that I could see the sea from my windows.

As I dreamed of freedom, I felt my box rise high into the air and then hurtle forward at great speed. From my windows I saw only clouds and sky, but I could hear the flapping of wings and presumed I had been snatched up by some great eagle. Then I felt my box falling until, with a huge splash, I landed in the sea.

I had been adrift for about four hours when I was picked up by a ship. I was so used to seeing monsters that I thought my rescuers were pygmies, rather than fellow Englishmen. The captain, hearing me utter such absurdities, thought I was raving. After I had slept, I was able to convince him of the truth of my story. I showed him some of my rarities: the comb I had made from the stubble of the King's beard, a length of the Queen's hair, and the four wasp stings. I gave the captain a footman's tooth as a gift. He asked me why I was always shouting and I explained it was a habit from living in Brobdingnag.

We landed in England on June 3rd, 1706. When I saw the littleness of everything I thought I was back in Lilliput, such is the power of habit and prejudice! It took me some time to adjust even to my family and friends who, like the captain, thought I had lost my wits. My wife protested that I should never return to sea again, but she had no power over what was to be my destiny. And here I end the second part of my unfortunate voyages.

From my windows I saw only clouds and sky, but I could hear the flapping of wings and presumed I had been snatched up by some great eagle.

Chapter three

A VOYAGE TO LAPUTA

A<small>FTER A NUMBER OF VISITS</small>, an old friend, Captain Robinson, persuaded me to join him as ship's surgeon on a voyage to the East Indies. My dear wife Mary eventually agreed, although I had only been at home three months. So, on August 5th, 1706 I set sail in the *Hopewell*.

We were about eleven days out from Tongking and to the northeast of Japan when we were boarded by pirates. My captain and fellow crew offered no resistance, so their lives were spared. As for me, my angry words and insults inflamed one of my captors, so as a punishment I was set adrift in a small boat. I had few provisions and only the possessions I had on me.

On my fifth day afloat I landed on a desolate island. While I was considering how miserable my end was likely to be, the sun was suddenly obscured by a vast opaque solid. It seemed about two miles up and hid the sun for six or seven minutes. As it came closer, I realized it was a huge flying island! On its sides I could make out stairways and galleries with people moving around. I waved and shouted until they noticed my distress. After a while, from the lowest gallery a seat was let down on a chain; I fastened myself in and was then drawn up by pulleys.

As it came closer, I realized it was a huge flying island!

I was escorted to the monarch of this flying island, which I discovered was named Laputa. His Majesty was seated behind a large table covered with globes, spheres, and mathematical instruments. He appeared to be deep in a problem and at first took no notice of me, until two servants each holding a bladder on a stick tapped him on the mouth and the right ear. As if waking from a dream, he suddenly became aware of me.

During my stay on Laputa, he proved a considerate host, allowed me to go where I wished, and arranged for me to receive instruction in their language and customs. I cannot say that I was ill treated, but the Laputians had no interest in me, nor anyone else, nor in anything other than mathematics, music, and astronomy. I have never met more disagreeable companions.

Piracy
The risk of being attacked by pirates was very real during the 18th century, when precious cargoes were often plundered by cutthroats. Gulliver and his crew were lucky to escape with their lives – pirates often murdered all witnesses so that news of their deeds died with them.

ALL ABOUT LAPUTA

Laputa is a floating island that hovers over the larger island of Balnibarbi. The King of Laputa is monarch of both islands. Although he lives on Laputa, his capital city, Laguda, is on Balnibarbi. Laputa relies on the earthbound land for food and wine, both of which are hauled up in baskets using a pulley system. Communication between the two islands is through messages sent up and down on long threads. Laputians are obsessed by music and mathematics, and do not have words to express the more practical things in life. Their clothes are decorated with mathematical symbols and musical instruments.

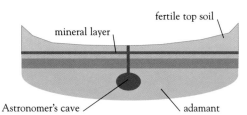

fertile top soil

mineral layer

Astronomer's cave

adamant

Cross-section of Laputa
The island mass is 300 yards (275 meters) deep. The upper layer consists of a fertile top soil and a substrata of minerals, but the base is a 200 yards thick layer of adamant – a legendary substance said to be impenetrable. The surface of Laputa slopes toward its center, where four large basins collect the rainwater for drinking.

Laputa

Balnibarbi

basins collecting rainwater

stairs to the different levels

entrance to the Astronomer's Cave

The island
Laputa is circular, 4½ miles (7 km) in diameter, and with a total surface area of 10,000 acres (4,050 hectares).

LAPUTIAN ODDITIES AND FLAPPERS

The Laputians spend their lives contemplating theories involving astronomy, mathematics, and music. Their heads are inclined to the side, with one eye turned inward and the other fixed on the heavens. Since they are constantly absorbed in abstract thought they need prompting to remind them of the presence of others. For this purpose, the rich employ flappers who carry a bladder filled with pebbles attached to the end of a stick. The flapper gently strikes his master's mouth if he has to be reminded to speak, or his ear if he has to listen.

Laputian women
Women of Laputa, unlike the men, do not have their heads in the clouds and are not absorbed in theories (so they have no need for flappers). Many women would prefer to leave the luxurious life on Laputa in favor of a more mundane freedom on the ground. However, for a woman to leave Laputa requires royal assent.

The stars, the sun, and their worries

Laputian astronomers have pinpointed 10,000 fixed stars, and can accurately calculate the movement of 93 comets. All Laputians worry that the Earth may be struck by a comet, or that the Sun will become dull and give no more light. Indeed their fears are so great that many people can't sleep at night.

Impracticalities

The Laputians have no practical abilities and in day-to-day life they are extremely clumsy. Their houses are ill-built, the walls slope and there are no right angles. They design their houses using complex geometric shapes, too complicated for the builders to understand.

Musical and mathematical references

The Laputian obsession with mathematics and music is even reflected in the way their food is prepared. Gulliver is served a shoulder of mutton that had been shaped into an equilateral triangle, a duck that had been trussed like a fiddle, and sausages and puddings made to resemble flutes and oboes. Servants cut the bread into cylinders, cones, or parallelograms.

roast duck shaped like a violin

A Laputian meal

ASTRONOMER'S CAVE AND THE LOADSTONE

At the center of Laputa there is access from the surface to a chasm that reaches about 100 yards (90 meters) into the adamant. At the bottom of the chasm there is a large dome, some 50 yards (45 meters) in diameter, which is known as Flandona Gagnole or the Astronomer's Cave. The cave is lit by 20 lamps, which are kept continually burning. Their strong light is reflected by the adamant walls and is thrown into every corner of the cave. Sextants, quadrants, telescopes, astrolabes, and other astronomical instruments are stored within the Astronomer's Cave, but its most important feature is an enormous loadstone.

astronomical equipment

The loadstone

the loadstone

The cave also houses a huge loadstone that is finely balanced on an axle. Laputa relies on this loadstone to move around the skies. One end of the stone is strongly attracted to the land of Balnibarbi below and, if it is turned downward, Laputa will be drawn toward the Earth. The other end of the stone is repelled by the land, so if this end is pointed downward, Laputa is forced to ascend into the sky. The island moves from side to side if the stone is at a slant. Laputa cannot move beyond the boundaries of Balnibarbi.

axle

Suppression of rebellion

On several occasions the subjects of Balnibarbi have rebelled against their Monarch in the sky, but these incidents have been suppressed in a number of ways. Options include Laputa hovering over the rebel region, depriving it of sun and rain; dropping heavy stones on it, or dropping the island on it. The last option would cause total destruction on the ground, damage the adamant, and immobilize Laputa.

After two months on Laputa, His Majesty permitted me to go down to the large island of Balnibarbi. I was lowered onto firm ground near the capital, Lagado, and there I stayed as the guest of Lord Munodi.

The next morning Lord Munodi and I made a tour of Lagado. All of the buildings were in ruins and the people walked around in rags, with expressions of despair written on their faces. The surrounding countryside was no different, being poorly cultivated, and the people toiling away with no apparent result.

Lord Munodi told me that this misery started forty years ago, after officials returned from Laputa, full of airy theories and ideas. They demanded a totally new way of living based on these theories, whereby all practical methods of living were not to be used. An Academy of Projectors was established in every town to think up ideas. But, so far, not one of these projects had worked in practice; and until they do the country waits in waste and misery.

One projector had been eight years trying to extract sunshine from cucumbers.

As a great admirer of new projects, I visited the grand Academy of Projectors in Lagado. Here there were at least five hundred rooms, and the projects were so numerous and diverse that I can only describe a few.

Irish peasantry
The misgoverned province of Balnibarbi is probably meant to be a portrait of Swift's native Ireland. Poverty and starvation were common in Ireland, and were sometimes a direct result of food being exported to mainland Britain.

From another room there came a horrible stink: a projector was trying to recycle human excrement into its original food.

Sir Isaac Newton
Newton (1642–1727), who is best known for discovering gravity, was President of the Royal Society from 1703 until his death. Many of the ludicrous experiments that appear in Gulliver's Travels are based on actual research carried out by the society in the 17th and 18th centuries.

One laboratory was full of cobwebs, in an experiment to get colored thread and cloth from spiders by feeding them colored flies.

One projector had been eight years trying to extract sunshine from cucumbers. He said that in another eight years he hoped to succeed. Unfortunately his stock of cucumbers was low, and he begged me for some money to buy more. Luckily Lord Munodi had given me some, knowing that the projectors were always begging from visitors.

From another room there came a horrible stink: a projector was trying to recycle human excrement into its original food. In another, I met an architect trying to build houses from the roof downward. One laboratory was full of cobwebs, in an experiment to get colored thread and cloth from spiders by feeding them colored flies.

After I had visited the department of speculative learning and the school of political projectors, I began to think of returning home to England. I traveled to Glubbdubdrib, then to the island of Luggnagg. From here I sailed to Japan and boarded a vessel for Amsterdam. On April 16th, 1710 I arrived in England to find my wife and family in good health. I had been absent for five years and six months.

Chapter four

A VOYAGE TO THE HOUYHNHNMS

Buccaneers

The extra crew that Gulliver takes on in Barbados turned out to be buccaneers. These were (often British) pirates who preyed upon Spanish ships. They were likely to mutiny, particularly if Gulliver wasn't a very good captain.

The Jolly Roger

The pirates' flag is black and displays a skull above cross-bones or crossed-swords. It would have been hoisted when a ship had been won by pirates.

IF ONLY I COULD HAVE LEARNED to know when I was happy. I had been at home with my wife and children for about five months when I accepted the advantageous post of captain of the *Adventure*, a stout merchantman. I left my poor wife, big with child, and set sail from Portsmouth on September 7th, 1710, bound for the South Seas.

Several men died of fever during the voyage, so I took on more crew in Barbados. I soon discovered that these rogues had previously been buccaneers, for they turned my crew against me and seized my ship. I was their prisoner for many weeks before they cast me ashore in some unknown land.

Feeling very desolate, I cautiously followed a track that headed inland. Before long I passed a field where I could just make out some strange creatures.

Their heads and breasts were covered in thick hair. They also had a long ridge of hair down their backs, and on their legs and feet; but the rest of their bodies was bare skin. The females were smaller than

the males and their bodies were covered in a sort
of down. They all had strong claws and, although
they moved on all-fours, they would often spring
and leap about on their hind legs, and were
nimble at climbing trees. On all my travels I had
never been so disgusted by a creature.

I carried on down the path, but was soon confronted by one of
these ugly animals. It lifted its forepaw toward me. As I had no wish
to injure the creature, I merely struck it with the flat of my sword.
The beast roared so loud that a herd of at least forty came flocking
about me, howling and making hideous faces. I ran to a tree and
there I kept them at bay, but several leapt into the branches and
discharged their excrement on my head.

Suddenly they turned and fled. I looked around to see what
could have caused this, but all I saw was a dapple-gray horse
walking quietly toward me.

*I ran to a tree and
there I kept them
at bay.*

The two horses looked me over carefully.

The horse looked at me, then examined my hands and feet, walking around me several times. We stood gazing at each other for some time; at last I reached out to stroke it but it shook its head and softly raised a forefoot to remove my hand.

Another horse, a brown bay, came up and they greeted each other by gently striking each other's right hooves and neighing. Then together, the two horses looked me over carefully. They gently felt my hat and my coat with their hoofs, and seemed particularly perplexed at my shoes and stockings.

They neighed frequently, which seemed to articulate their thoughts. I heard the word "*Yahoo*" several times. So, in a clear voice, I imitated "*Yahoo*." Both were visibly surprised, and the brown bay tried me with a more difficult word, "*Houyhnhnm*." After he had prompted me a few times, I managed to say "*Houyhnhnm*." They seemed amazed. The two horses then parted, and the gray indicated that I should walk with him.

When we arrived at a long, low building made of timber and with a straw-covered roof, I expected to encounter some people. Instead, inside there were not only five horses sitting on their haunches, but also others doing domestic work. They neighed several times to each other before I was taken to another room where a comely mare, with a colt and a foal, was sitting on a straw mat.

The mare examined me closely. Then she looked at me contemptuously and said, "*Yahoo*." I was led outside across a courtyard to a building where there were three of those filthy creatures I had seen before. They were tied around the neck to a beam and were eating roots and the carcass of some diseased animal. They held their food between the claws of their forefeet and tore it with their teeth.

The largest of these beasts was led into the yard and placed beside me. We were carefully compared, and again I heard the word "*Yahoo*." To my horror, apart from my clothes and this creature's hairiness and nails, our bodies were no different.

A sorrel nag offered me some stinking ass's flesh, which I politely declined. I also shook my head at offers of roots and hay and oats. After believing that I might well starve, I luckily spotted a passing cow. I pointed to it and was brought a large bowl of milk, which well refreshed me.

The World Turned Upside Down
This illustration is from a well-known 17th-century poem called The World Turned Upside Down, *which was read by the young Swift. Several illustrations to the poem, which had a strong influence on Gulliver's* Travels, *show horses bossing humans around.*

The mare examined me closely. Then she looked at me contemptuously and said, "Yahoo."

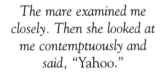

Cruelty to horses
Horses and ponies were bred to work during the 18th century. Often they were badly fed and forced to pull very heavy loads. If they stumbled they were whipped. Once they were too old or sick to work, they were sent to the knacker's yard, where they were slaughtered.

The master of the household allowed me to live and eat separately from the Yahoos. He suspected that I must be one of these brutes, but my civility, cleanliness, and eagerness to learn were the very opposite to them. For awhile I successfully hid the fact that my clothes were a false covering, but early one morning my master saw me sleeping without them. I admitted that the reason for my secrecy was that I wished to distinguish myself from the Yahoos. Although he was now convinced that I must be one, I begged him not to reveal my secret, nor call me Yahoo, and he graciously agreed to both of these requests.

I was eager to learn their language and to prove that, unlike the Yahoos, I was a rational being. My master and his family tutored me and, after three months, I was able to hold a conversation. My master could not believe that I had come from a country beyond the sea, where Yahoos were capable of building boats. He asked if there were Houyhnhnms in my country.

I told him we had great numbers of Houyhnhnms, which we called horses; but that Yahoos were the governing species. I then described how horses were trained for various kinds of hard work and our way of riding them using a bridle and saddle. Some lucky horses, I explained, were well cared for until they became old or ill, when they were sold and forced to do all kinds of drudgery until they died. Their skins were stripped off and their bodies eaten or left to rot. Other, less lucky horses were forced to work like slaves all their lives until they dropped.

My master, after showing great indignation at this cruel treatment, said he would rather talk about other differences between our two countries and in particular of our politics, including the many reasons that we went to war. I also told him about our legal system and how frequently injustice was done in the name of the law. My master commented that it was a great pity that lawyers and judges, who were clever men, if I was to be believed, could not use their intelligence to instruct others in wisdom and knowledge.

Houyhnhnms and Yahoos

The country of the Houyhnhnms is an island in the South Seas. By small boat it is four to five days west of New Holland (Australia). The dominant species is a race of gentle and rational horses known as the Houyhnhnms, which means "Perfection of Nature" in their language. The Yahoos are wild creatures that look like Neanderthal Man. The Houyhnhnms keep them in kennels.

Houyhnhnms' Land

Houyhnhnms

An unshod horse's hoof

The Houyhnhnms use the hollow part of their fore-hoofs in the same way as we use our hands. They can milk cows, make earthenware pots, and weave straw mats. Tools are made from flint, since metal is unknown.

• They are governed by reason, and lead peace-loving and crime-free lives.

• The write fine poetry on benevolence, race-winning, and friendship.

• They live in long, low buildings with thatched roofs and large rooms with clay floors.

• They do not suffer from disease and do not need doctors.

• Most horses live for 70 or 80 years. Before they die, they say "goodbye" to their friends.

• Both sexes have the same education, based on industry, exercise, and cleanliness.

• They have no written language; theirs is an oral tradition.

• Couples marry for life. They only have two foals to prevent overpopulation.

Yahoos

Yahoos resemble humans, although they are hairier and usually travel on all-fours. They are amonge the most unpleasant creatures on Earth, loving nastiness and filth.

• They are cunning, treacherous, revengeful, and cowardly.

• Because they are strong, they are used as beasts of burden.

• They live in groups; the ugliest qualifies as leader.

• They eat anything raw, from roots to dead dogs.

• They suffer from sickness and disease.

• They are unable to speak.

• They do not form permanent relationships with the opposite sex.

Neanderthal Man

Highwaymen

Making a journey was often dangerous in 18th-century Britain, when highwaymen would attack coaches and rob the occupants.

Sir Robert Walpole addressing his cabinet.

Politicians

Sleaze in politics is nothing new. Politicians in Sir Robert Walpole's government openly worked to advance their own interests and were known to bribe or threaten voters.

Mr. Smith as Plume in *The Beaux Stratagem* by George Farquhar

A Wit

A wit was a man who used words in a clever or humorous way, and was a stock character in comedies of the time. There were some genuine wits in society, but most thought they were much funnier than they really were.

I settled down happily in this land, enjoyed the favor of my master and had perfect health in body and tranquillity of mind. My life was free from bribery, flattery, fraud, oppression, and lies. Here there were no gallows, censurers, backbiters, pickpockets, robbers, highwaymen, lawyers, politicians, wits, tedious talkers, leaders, cheats, or murderers. There was no pride nor vanity; no fops, nobility, bullies, or drunkards. When I thought of my family, my friends, my countrymen, or the human race in general, I saw them as they really were: Yahoos. I was even revolted by my own appearance and tried in every way to be more of a Houyhnhnm, this most wise and honorable of all races.

In the midst of all my happiness, my master sent for me. I sensed his reluctance to tell me his news. After a short silence he told me that the Representative Council considered me a threat to their way

*I took leave of
my master
and lady.*

of life. As I was a Yahoo with some intelligence, they feared I might incite a Yahoo uprising. To guard against this, they proposed that either I must live and work as a Yahoo, or swim back to my own country.

I collapsed with the utmost grief and despair, for I knew that, however I pleaded, the Houyhnhnms would not be shaken by my arguments. I had no alternative but to respect their wisdom and the sound reasons for their decision. I could not bear the thought of living among the Yahoos. The alternative of returning to my country, where I would degenerate into the vices and corruptions of my own species of Yahoo, was equally horrible.

I decided to build a boat. Within two months all was ready, and the sad day came. I took leave of my master and lady, my eyes flowing with tears and my heart sunken with grief. I began my desperate voyage on February 15th, 1715 and, as the shore retreated behind me, I could just hear the cry, *"Hnuy illa nyha maiah Yahoo,"* "Take care of yourself, gentle Yahoo."

They gazed in amazement at my strange appearance.

I was hoping to find some small island where I could spend my life in solitude, but my small boat was blown due east until I was sighted by a Portuguese ship. I had no wish to be rescued by European Yahoos and protested strongly, but I was such a curiosity that they bound me up and bundled me on board. They gazed in amazement at my strange appearance, for, as my clothes had worn out, I had made myself a coat of skins, wooden-soled shoes, and fur stockings to distinguish myself from the naked Yahoos.

The sailors spoke to me and, although they understood my replies, they fell about laughing saying that I sounded like a whinnying horse. The captain, who was called Pedro de Mendez, showed me every kindness, but I replied rudely to him, finding it impossible to conceal my revulsion for human beings. I felt faint with their smell, could not eat their food, and spent most of the voyage to Lisbon alone in my cabin.

In Lisbon I lodged with the captain and, thanks to his patience, my terror of people gradually lessened. By degrees, I was able to move about the house, then peep through the windows, and then I let the captain walk me in the streets. Eventually he persuaded me to return to my family, where I could be as reclusive as I wished within my own house.

On December 5th, 1715 I arrived home to the great joy of my wife and children, who had thought I was dead. I must confess that, as my thoughts were still on the Houyhnhnms, the sight of my family filled me with disgust and contempt.

❧

It is now five years since I returned home. I have become more tolerant and can now eat in the same room as my family, yet still I cannot bear them to hold my hand. I keep two young horses and talk with them for four hours each day. They understand me tolerably well, and we have a great friendship.

And so, dear reader, I have come to the end of the true and accurate account of my sixteen years of traveling. Instead of astonishing and amusing you with strange and improbable tales, I have chosen to write the plain facts in the simplest manner, about places I have visited and the things I have seen. All along my intention has been to inform rather than merely entertain.

Hating humankind
Some people have seen the ending of Gulliver's Travels as a sign that Swift, like Gulliver, had grown to hate the human race. It is more likely, however, that he is making fun of Gulliver for being so self-righteous and pompous. The book's final image of Gulliver chatting to his horses while ignoring his own family is a foolish one.

I keep two young horses and talk with them for four hours each day.

Swift and Gulliver

J onathan Swift was born in Dublin in 1667, the son of English parents. He was educated at Kilkenny Grammar School and Trinity College, Dublin. When there was a Catholic uprising in Ireland in the late 1680s, Swift – who was a Protestant – moved to England and became secretary to Sir William Temple. In 1694, Swift became a Church of Ireland priest, and later he was made Dean of St. Patrick's Cathedral in Dublin. He was often bad tempered, but fought tirelessly against war and poverty, and tried to improve life for the people of Ireland. *Gulliver's Travels*, his most famous work, was published in 1726. During his lifetime Swift suffered from a nervous illness. He was declared insane in 1742, and died three years later.

Jonathan Swift 1667–1745

Dublin

Dublin in the late 17th and early 18th centuries was a vicious and corrupt place. Most people were trapped in poverty, unable to improve their lives because of the restrictive Penal Laws. Later, during the Georgian period, Dublin became an elegant and lively city.

18th-century Dublin

London

During Swift's lifetime, London became the world's biggest city – a vital commercial center at the heart of the expanding British Empire. But disease soon became a problem in the overcrowded streets.

18th-century London

Book editions

Swift started writing *Gulliver's Travels* in 1714, and it was published anonymously in 1726. Since then numerous editions have been produced of the classic tale. Swift was paid £200 for *Gulliver* – the only money he ever received for his writing.

"The King's dwarf plays Gulliver a trick" (illustration from 1803)

Gulliver and the Lilliputian army (illustration from 1882)

Gulliver confronted by the Yahoos (illustration from c.1919)

Alexander Pope

Swift's most famous contemporary was the poet Alexander Pope (1688–1744). The son of a Catholic linen merchant, Pope was crippled by disease as a boy, and never grew more than 4½ feet (137 cm) tall. This, combined with his religion, meant that he was always seen as an outsider. Pope's most famous work is the *Rape of the Lock*, but he is also known for his political satires. He was a member of the Scriblerus Club, with Swift and John Gay.

Portrait of Alexander Pope, 1722

House of Commons

From the Reformation until the Palace of Westminster burned down in 1834, the House of Commons was situated in St. Stephen's Chapel. The government and opposition sat facing one another, while many nominally independent MPs moved around the House.

The Whigs, who held power for much of the 18th century, were the forerunners of today's Liberals.

The Tories were today's Conservatives.

The House of Commons in session (1710)

London coffeehouses

Swift had access to a huge reading public who met in London's 3,000-plus coffeehouses. These buildings acted as centers where people could gossip, exchange ideas, and read the latest journals, such as *The Tatler* and *The Spectator*.

GULLIVER THROUGH THE AGES

Because it works on so many different levels – as a political satire, a travel book, and a fairy tale – the story of Gulliver has captured the imaginations of generations of readers of all ages. Many of the issues that angered Swift, such as war, poverty, and lack of equality and access to education, are just as relevant today as they were 300 years ago. For these reasons, Gulliver's Travels has remained popular. But, unlike many other classics, the story has proved difficult to translate to the stage because it involves a race of tiny people, giants, a flying island, and talking horses. With the advent of film and television, and the increasing use of animation and computer technology, good adaptations are being made possible for the first time.

Gulliver pulling the fleet, in the 1939 animated version of Gulliver's Travels

Gulliver, played by Richard Harris, captured by Lilliputians

Cinematic versions

Films in the late 20th century tried to capture different aspects of Gulliver's personality. In the 1976 version, Richard Harris portrayed him as the adventurous hero. But, during the late 1990s, Ted Danson showed Gulliver locked up in a lunatic asylum. Swift, who was declared insane at the end of his life, left money in his will for Dublin's first lunatic asylum to be built.

Ted Danson, as Gulliver, looking through the window of the Lilliputian royal palace

Acknowledgements

Picture Credits
The publishers would like to thank the following for their
kind permission to reproduce the photographs.
t=top, b=bottom, l=left, r=right, a=above

AKG London: 57cr, 62bra
Bridgeman Art Library: 9tr, 10l,
12tl, 15br, 16tl, b, 17tr, 19tr, 22tl,
33br, 35tr, 36cl, 38bl, 40bl, 41tr,
42b, 43br, 47cr, 50bl, 51tr, 52tl,
55tr, 56-7b, 58tl, cl, 62-3
(background), 62cl, cb, bl, cr, 63tl
ET Archive: 23tr
Mary Evans Picture Library:
16c, 27tr, 41cr, 43t, 56tl, 58bl,
62br, 63tr
Ronald Grant Archive: 6-7, 24bl,
44tl, 63cra, crb, b
National Trust Photo Library: 43tr
Gregory K Scott: 25bra

Additional photography by: Tina
Chambers, Andy Crawford, Dave
King, Matthew Ward

**Dorling Kindersley would
particularly like to thank the
following people:**
Tanya Tween for design assitance;
Laia Roses for jacket design;
Jill Bunyan for DTP design;
Linda Dare for Production
assistance; Kate Duncan for picture
research; Sally Hamilton in DK
Picture Library.